In loving memory to Viola Cloretta Jeffrey, Harriette Ruth Bardfeld, and all parents who teach their children that skin color is not important; what really matters is the way people make you feel.

This book is dedicated to Megan, Nicole, Noah, and my son Dennis Jeffrey II in hopes that they grow up and see the beauty in everyone.

Special thanks to my wife Abby because without her, this book and our son would not be possible.

e Abby and Noah helping their mom bake.
ey can read all the directions to make a great cake.

ey are smart because they know how to measure and pour,
d you can smell the yummy baked goods right through the door.

e Abby and Noah helping their neighbors shovel snow.
hen asked for help, it's hard for them to say no.
ey are good neighbors and excellent friends,
d they will help you through to the very end.

eir skin tone is white and they have straight blonde hair.
ey like how they look and can fit in anywhere.
ey are not only good to others, but they are also very smart,
d they love their family and friends with all their heart.

e Breona and Keanu helping daddy cook.
ey love how each dish has a different look.

ey are smart because they read books, some on cooking,
ome on stars,
d especially ones about adventures near and far.

e Breona and Keanu walking the dog of a sick friend.
ey made her a card with good wishes to send.
ey are kind to animals and considerate of others.
/ou met them you could tell they're sister and brother.

eir skin tone is dark brown and they have curly black hair.
ey like how they look and can fit in anywhere.
ey are not only good to others, but they are also very smart,
d they love their family and friends with all their heart.

e Juan and Ana reading a map to the zoo.
ey're excited because there's lots of animals to view.

ey are smart because they know how to read a map,
d they will always be able to find places in a snap.

e Juan and Ana helping a person cross the street.
ey are nice and kind to everyone they meet.

eir skin tone is light brown and they have dark brown hair.
ey like how they look and can fit in anywhere.
ey are not only good to others, but they are also very smart,
d they love their family and friends with all their heart.

e Takumi and Sayuri reading the menu for lunch.
ey know how to read what's available to munch.

ey are smart because they count the change on their own,
d save enough money for an ice cream cone.

e Takumi and Sayuri hold open the door.
ce kids like them will definitely soar.
ey are considerate kids and they are always polite.
 if you were to sneeze, they would say gesundheit!

eir skin tone is light tan and they have straight black hair.
ey like how they look and can fit in anywhere.
ey are not only good to others, but they are also very smart,
d they love their family and friends with all their heart.

e all eight together in the school playground,
ding and swinging, and running all around.

ey like each other because of what's inside,
d no one needs to feel bad or run and hide.

e live on one planet; we are one world, one race.
e human race comes in many shades, just look at each face.

ch person is different, and that's ok,
cause everyone is beautiful in his or her own way!

About the Author

Dennis Robert Jeffrey was born in Bronx, New York, to first generation Caribbean parents. His beliefs of diversity and inclusion were initially formed by his parents, and reinforced by his educational settings.

Dennis' educational settings were racially diverse, ranging from predominately white (elementary school), to racially mixed (middle school and high school), to predominately black (Morgan State University Undergraduate Studies), to predominately white (Carnegie-Mellon University Graduate Studies).

For twenty eight years, Dennis worked for Metropolitan Life Insurance Company in New York City before retiring as an Assistant Vice President to become a stay-at-home dad.

His first book, "It's Beautiful to Be Different and Being Different is Beautiful," is a lesson in diversity, inclusion, self awarenes, and self love. This book seeks to demonstrate that we all live on one planet, and that people of all ethnicities are beautiful, smart, and good hearted. Additionally, every group across the globe should teach its children the important lesson of self love and diversity. Dennis believes that all parents should raise their children to be devoid of racial misconceptions, stereotypes or stigmas.

Printed in the U.S.A.
Library of Congress Control Number: 2011911292
ISBN (13) Number: 978-1466364288
ISBN (10) Number: 1466364289